THE NAUGHTY BAWDY
MUSIC HOUR

Also by ESMERALDA LINTNER

THE GANJA NETWORK 2

THE ELEGANCE OF LIFE

GABRIELLE'S HEART
An Angel's Touch

FIFI'S EROTIC BOUTIQUE
A Store of Pleasure

LINCOLN MEETS WASHINGTON
An Historical Fantasy

FIFI'S NAUGHTY RHYMES and FAIRY TALES
Make Believe Erotica

FIF'S NAUGHTY RHYMES and FAIRY TALES
Volumes 2 and 3

TRUMP: THE PRINCE OF FOOLS
A Musical Fantasy

TEDDY, HARRY and DICK
The Presidents Speak

LADY FARTINGHAM
An Historical Tale in
Flatulent Taste

REVEREND STIFFWILLY
A Heavenly Endowment

TWO-TIMING TILLIE
Femme Fatale

THE SHADOW OF FALSE FACE

A GHOUL'S DELIGHT
Full of Fiedish Fun

MONIQUE'S PLEASURE PALACE
Zany & Erotic Fun

THE WACKY WHACKING-OFF WORLD OF SEX
Naughty & Bawdy Antics

THE NAUGHTY BAWDY MUSIC HOUR

by

ESMERALDA LINTNER

With many illustrations and photos

(Curtain rises. Out walks a man wearing a jock strap and a pair of glittery glasses in rainbow colors. His eyes bulge, literally pop out. Waving a long cigarette holder and taking a dainty puff, he begins speaking to an audience)

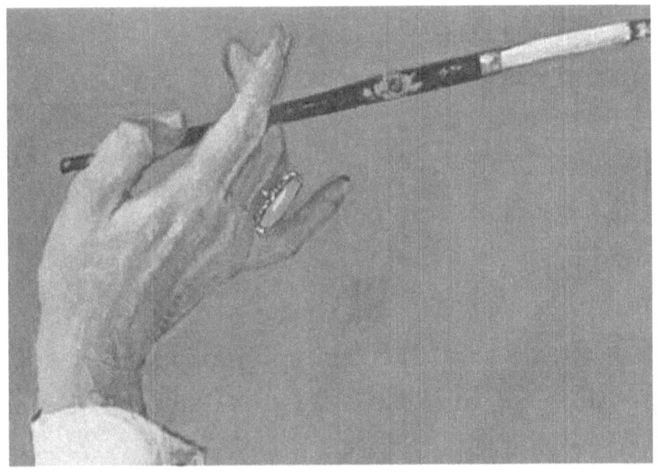

Hello there, everybody. Allow me to introduce myself. I am none other than Peeping Pecker Pete. I shall be your host for this naughty, bawdy music hour. To start us off, here are those bad little boys themselves who will sing their latest hit song, "Yank That Doodle Dandy." They call themselves the Continental Patriotic Quartet. Let's put our hands together and give them a warm welcome!

(Four youngsters in Revolutionary War outfits trot onto the stage, waving a Betsy Ross flag as they strut)

YANK THAT DOODLE, DANDY

Yankee Doodle rode into town,
Wore riding chaps on his pony,
He grabbed his cock
Hard as a rock
"By God," he cried,
"It's lookin' rather bony!"

Yankee Doodle, keep it up
Yank that Doddle, Dandy
If you jerk it long enough
You'll have some cream-filled candy.

I went down by the riverside
Where naked boys were swimmin',
Their peckers stuck out
Hard as rocks
I wonder what they're doin'?
"Come on in, and join the fun,
We're patriotically screwin'!"

Yankee Doodle, keep it up
Yank that Doodle, Dandy
If you jerk it long enough
You'll have some cream-filled candy.

(PEEPING PECKER PETE emerges onstage once again to address the audience) Wasn't that fantastic, ladies and gentlemen? Good ol' "Yank That Doodle Dandy," a real patriotic song for young and old to cherish forever. And now we bring on the next big act. Wet your whistle, boys and girls, and get nice and loaded, because our good ol' drinking buddies themselves, The Tavern Boys, are gonna delight you with their latest and, you'll agree, greatest hit, "The Pride of His Big Wee-Wee." Give 'em a big hand to jerk off, my friends! **(AUDIENCE giggles as THE TAVERN BOYS enter to sing)**

THE PRIDE OF HIS BIG WEE-WEE

There was a young lad,
So goes the story I was told,
He was not very brave
Nor very bold.

Till one day he reached down
To touch his britches,
He looked down
And fell on the ground,
Laughing himself in stitches.

"Holy shit! Christ!
Look how it's coming out!
I have myself one big
Water spout!"

It was from the Pride of
His Big wee-wee,
The Pride of His Big Wee-wee.
It shook and it jiggled
As he gave it a wiggle
It was from the Pride of
His Big Wee-wee.

He displayed it,
Walked round town for all to see.
People came from far and wide
To get a glimpse of his
Big Wee-wee.

CHORUS: Wee-wee
Wee-wee
It was the Pride of His Big Wee-wee.
It shook
And it jiggled
As he gave it a wiggle
The Pride of His Big Wee-wee.

ALL CLAP TOGETHER:
It shook
It jiggled,
He gave it a wiggle,
The Pride of His Big Wee-wee.

Now he's not so timid
And not so shy.

When you see him
His Big Wee-wee will catch your eye
It's from the Pride of His Big Wee-wee.

(Repeat CHORUS)

It shook
It jiggled,
He gave it a wiggle,
The Pride of His Big Wee-Weeeeee!!!

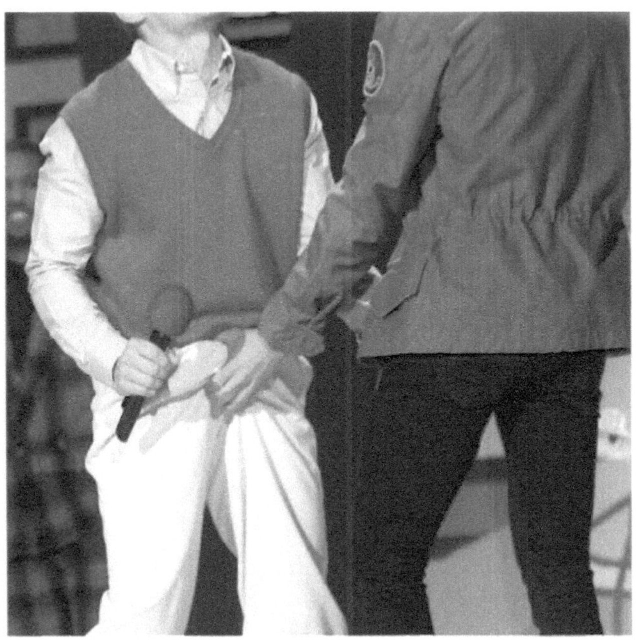

(PECKER PEEEPING PETE returns to the stage, waving off THE TAVERN BOYS as they attempt to take a final bow after the rousing applause from the AUDIENCE. He is dressed differently than before, wearing a lacey buckskin shirt atop his jockstrap) I just love the old-fashioned way of dressing. Get a load of this character coming onto our stage for the next number: decked out in a Medieval doublet and over-robe. He looks like some kind o' actor from a Shakespeare play, don't'cha think? Anyhoo, let's give this dime-store Romeo a huge welcome as he sings his newest hit, "The Heavenly Poker." Here he is in all his glory, ladies and gentlemen, The Tripping Troubadour!

THE HEAVENLY POKER

Come stroll on over
To the heavenly clover
Come, lay young maidens
On feathery down.

Roll them on over,
Stroke,
Show them your poker,
Poke them as you nail them
On feathery down.

They'll love the stiff poker
As you poke with your poker

You'll make them
feel as if on a
    heavenly
       cloud.

It will make them
    scream happy,
It'll make you fee
    quite proud.
Stroll on over
To the heavenly
    clover
The maidens on
heavenly down.

Oh, roll them over,
Stroke, show them
    your poker,
Poke them as you
    nail them....

On fea-ther-ry doooo-oooowwwwn!

(final flourish with vibrating strings from cello
followed by wild applause and cheers from the
AUDIENCE)

(HOST dances back onstage and does a pirouette which causes the AUDIENCE to titter uncontrollably. Regaining his balance and signaling for the audience members to hush, he continues with his hosting duties) Hi there, y'all! How y'all doin'? If you're wondering why I've suddenly turned all cornpone on y'all, it's because our next number is a real down home country song direct from them hills out yonder thar --- yuck yuck! Here are your favorite hillbillies and mine, The Hootenanny Hollerers, performing their big hit, "Diddly-Down-Down."

DIDDLY-DOWN-DOWN

I love when they use the old lips
Make me feel free as a clown
They would give it jerk
While making a smirk

I love it when they went down on my shaft.
Love the feeling when they went
Down, down, diddly-down-down
Oh, how I love when they went down on me!

The lips were all wrapped
Feeling tight as can be,
Oh, how I love the feeling when they went
Down, down, diddly-down-down,
When they went down on me.

They stroked it, even nibbled on it,
Holy shit, it was swell!
Until a big gusher came squirting out,
It was that magic mouth going in and out.

It was from going
Down, down, diddly-down-down,
I love when they went
Down, down, diddly-down-down,
How I love when they went down on me.

(PEEPING PECKER TOM returns to the stage, waving off the HOOTENANNY HOLLERERS who are still dancing and prancing around. The HOST is wearing a cap and gown, similar to the garments of a graduating student) You in the audience here in the studio as well as out in TV land all know my love and respect for education. With that in mind, I take great pleasure in presenting Doctor Fatty Know-It-All, our resident brain, with a timely little number entitled "Three Words." Let's respectfully applaud him as the pompous fool waddles onto our stage! (AUDIENCE giggles once again and they clap lightly as instructed)

THREE WORDS

I have just learned three words
That bring you much relief and laughter.
Come, listen and see,
They bring much joy to you and me.

They are FART,
FIDDLE
And FORNICATE!

These three words, they be

10

FART,
FIDDLE,
FORNICATE:
Fun for you and me!

Now, these three words are simple:
They'll leave you in stitches
            a'layin' on the ground.
FART,
   FIDDLE,
      FORNICATE;
They'll leave you howlin'
            like a hound!

These are the magic words of the day.
Remember:
FART,
   FIDDLE,
      FORNICATE ---
They're fun for you and me.
FART,
   FIDDLE,
      FORNICATE ---
Great for you and me.

Now these three words are simple:
Simple as A B C.
Come and join me
          and you will see.
They are
FART,
    FIDDLE,
        and FORNICATE;
Come all together and
          join the fun.

They are
FART,
    FIDDLE,
        FORNICATE ---
Let's repeat them once again:
FART,
    FIDDLE,
        FORNICATE ---
There! You got it!
They're here for you and me!

(FATTY takes a bow and almost gets stuck in that position because of his enormous girth. STAGEHANDS step in to help him off stage and out of camera range. Host PEEPING PECKER PETE shakes his head as he comes back onstage.) I guess that ol' Fatty Know-It-All will be out of commission for a while. I told the big slob to lose a couple pounds, but he ignored my advice. Oh well... (HOST removes a package of condoms from his pocket and shows it to the AUDIENCE) I always like to carry a little protection with me wherever I go, y'know what I mean? The next act we're gonna hear is a man who is exactly what the doctor ordered for such occasions: none other than Professor Cornhole the First. He' s gonna belt out a song he wrote himself, and it's called "Prophylactic Rubber Condoms." Let's slip one on for him!

PROPHYLACTIC RUBBER CONDOMS

**Men, gather round!
There's something you need to hear
And see!
Every man needs one,
It's great for you and me.
You'll love it;
Feels great!
For pleasure and protection**

How happy you will be!
That pride and joy of yours
Hanging down below your knees!
We call them
Prophylactic Rubber
                    Condoms,
Yes, it's those Prophylactic Rubber
                    Condoms,
        Ready for when you cum!

They're stretchy,
Elastic,
That heavenly ecclesiastic
        Prophylactic Rubber Condoms.

Yes, indeed!
Those Prophylactic Rubber Condoms.
        They're ready when you cum!

And they come in assorted flavors ---
Lubricated or not, whichever you like!
They feel great,
They do the job!

Just ask Bill or Mike!

They love their
Prophylactic Rubber
        Condoms.
Yesiree, those
        Prophylactic Rubber
                Condoms:
They're ready for when you cum!

So men,
Wrap and stretch them
Around the old pole or pecker,
Whatever you care to call it is
        OK by me!
Be sure to wear one,
And how happy you will be!
It's those Prophylactic Rubber
                Condoms,
The one and only Prophylactic Rubber
                Condoms,
They're ready when you cum!

(HOST applauds PROFESSOR CORNHOLE THE FIRST with as much enthusiasm as the AUDIENCE) I can't tell you how much I enjoy songs with a message, ladies and gentlemen. Our next group guarantees they'll keep your ship afloat. They call themselves The Four Horny Sailors, and boy! do they ever live up to their name! Here's their latest hit which is shooting up the charts like a speeding bullet: "Drop The Pill Down."

DROP THE PILL DOWN

I'm looking over the girl's
    big fat tummy
That I forgot to prevent one day
Now I'm looking over a baby
    that's comin'
My God, it's the fifth one
    on its way!

I hear the angels a-drummin'
And singin' me this song:

Drop the pill down, lassie,

Drop the pill down,
Woe, ho, drop the pill down ---

No more new babies,
Laddies or lasses,
If you tell her to drop the pill down,
Woe, ho, drop the pill down ---

It will prevent them from
        getting too fat
And having a birth,
It'll give her much girth
If you tell her to
        drop the pill down,
Woe, ho, drop the pill down!

You'll be so happy
By not giving birth to
        your new pappy!
Drop the pill down, lassie,
Woe, ho, drop the pill down ---

(Host **PEEPING PECKER PETE** returns to the stage, fanning himself and wiping his brow) Whew! Do those sailor boys ever turn me on and make my peckers stand at attention --- ahoy, mateys! Gosh Almighty and shiver me timbers, bucko! (**AUDIENCE snickers**) Now then, since I regained my composure and my damn pecker is flaccid once again, I can introduce this next act, and is it ever a doozy! Everyone loves the class clown, right, gang? With that in mind, it's time to introduce a genuine comic, a real jolly joker if ever there was one. Let's give a hearty round of applause for Jackie the Jerk-Off Jester. He's gonna charm the pants off us with his brand new hit, hot off the record presses, and it's called "Hey Fiddle Fiddle." (**HOST cup his hands, locks his arms and swings them like a baseball player stepping up to bat**) Hit it, Jackie Baby!

HEY FIDDLE FIDDLE

**Hey Fiddle Fiddle
Let's feel fiddle tonight,
The moon is bright,
Feeling nice and tight
To fiddle with me tonight.**

**Hey Fiddle Fiddle
Let's feel and fiddle tonight!
In goes a finger
Once or twice,**

Oh, how it's feeling
Mighty nice!
As we both fiddle, fiddle,
Let's feel fiddle tonight.

I give my finger
A wiggle
As we feel fiddle tonight.
Wiggle, jiggle,
Feel fiddle,
It's alright.

As we fiddle, fiddle,
Feel fiddle tonight.

(**HOST is still bouncing to the rhythmic beat of the previous musical number as he jiggles back onstage**) I have heard lots of nutty, off-the-wall songs in my time, but here's a group whose latest musical numbers beats 'em all. "Pop Goes The Wee-Wee," performed by none other than those nutty, off-the-wall bunch of screwballs themselves, The Screwballs!

POP! GOES THE WEE-WEE

All around the satin lavender bed
He was being chased by a wee-wee.
He finally got caught
How hard it stuck out
Then pop! goes the wee-wee.

They finally stuck it in
Then pop! went the wee-wee.

All the night
They were chased by a wee-wee.
They finally got caught
By this big hanging thing,
When they got stuck with it
And pop! goes the wee-wee.

(HOST reappears onstage) What would a naughty, bawdy music hour be without a classic song which is beloved by our entire community? I'm referring to that classic which was first sung in the vintage movie, *The Wizard of Scuzz* --- none other than "Over the Gay Rainbow." And here to present his version of this much heralded musical number, I have the distinct honor of welcoming a vocalist of great renown --- none other than your favorite and mine, Michael Hungnutter! **(wild applause, cheers and whistling from AUDIENCE)**

OVER THE GAY RAINBOW

**Somewhere over the Gay Rainbow
Nude boys fly,
Boys fly over the Gay Rainbow,
Why, oh why the fuck can't I?**

**Where you bang your cherry,
Bang your cock,
Where you bite on tall, huge lemon cocks,
That's where you'll find me ----**

**Somewhere over the Gay Rainbow
Nude boys fly,
Boys fly over the Gay Rainbow,
Why, oh why the fuck can't I?**

**Where pools of cum, cumming rivers flow,
How much cumming, I don't know,
It's where you'll find me ---**

Somewhere over the Gay
Rainbow
Nude boys fly,
Boys fly over that Gay Rainbow,
Why (**sniff**)
Oh why (**sniff sniff**)
Why the fuck can't I?

Where's there chocolate
With cherry nuts,
With big creamy
Shining bubble butts,
That's where I'll be tasting ----

Somewhere over the Gay Rainbow
Nude boys still fly,
Boys continue flying over that damn Gay Rainbow,
So why in the name of all the flying fucks
Can't I?!?

Just the thought of it makes me hot,
Makes me feel like cumming a lot,
I can't wait to screw there ---

Somewhere over the kinky Gay Rainbow
Those big-dicked hunky boys fly,
Muscle-bound, tight-assed boys still fly over
That fuck-fest filled Gay Rainbow,
So tell me, you assholes, why oh why
Can't a measly little cornholer, (that's what I am)
Can't I?

(**HOST returns to the stage, hanky in hand and shedding huge puddles of tears**) Wasn't that a moving experience, ladies and gentlemen? ***sniff*** Forgive me for being so emotional --- that song breaks me up every time I hear it. (**HOST blows his nose so noisily, it sounds like a trombone sounding off**) Okay, okay, enough of this bullshit sentimentality. On with the show, as they say in the biz! You know, friends, I just love listening to a live band. Here's a guy who always strikes up the music wherever he goes. Leading his own seventy-six piece band, here's the Master Band Leader himself. You all know him and love him. Ladies and Gentlemen, I offer for your approval none other than your favorite and mine, The Big Boner! Feel free to join him in singing his all-time great hit, "Seventy-Six Hard Ones."

SEVENTY-SIX HARD ONES

Seventy-six hard ones wagging in the air
With a hundred and twenty-one bare butts,
Some with hair ---
You will see them all wagging in tune
You will see them stiffen with pride,
Sticking way up high,
Don't get too close
For they may hit you in the eye
As they go by....

They're from the
Seventy-six hard ones wagging in the air
With a hundred and twenty-one bare butts,
    Some with hair ----
The dicks are happy, proud and free,
Nice and stiff as they face you and me.

They're from the
Seventy-six hard ones wagging in the air
With a hundred and twenty-one bare butts,
    Some with hair ----
When you see them you'll turn nice and
    hard yourself

They're from the
Seventy-six hard ones wagging in the air
With a hundred and twenty-one bare butts,
    Some with hair ---
When you see them they'll make you nice and hot,
Your cocks may be dancing quite a lot.

They're from those
Seventy-six hard ones wagging in the air
With a hundred and twenty-one bare butts,
    Some with hair ----
So c'mon, join the fun,
Wave your hard ones,
Shake your buns,
And you'll sing this song forevermore with me

All together now! (AUDIENCE joins merrily in
singing the now familiar refrain)
Seventy-six hard ones wagging in the air
With a hundred and twenty-one bare butts,
    Some with hair ----

(CHORUS continues until music fades and
performer leaves the stage to a standing ovation. It
turns out to be a true show-stopping number!)

(Host PEEPING PECKER PETE returns to the stage, this time having changed into a priest's robe and raising his hands in praise) Let's keep up the pace of this program, but get ourselves a whole bunch of good religion. I just love me a good dose of heavenly, inspirational songs ev'ry so often. Here's a group who'll take you right into the presence of the angels and all the heavenly hosts. Ladies and Gentlemen, to inspire you and give you spiritual comfort, it gives me great pleasure to welcome The Hallelujah Perverts. They'll belt out that monster hit of theirs, "Dem Hard Bones."

DEM HARD BONES

Dem bones,
Dem hard bones,
Dem bones,
Dem hard bones,
I get a real stiff hard bone
When my boner becomes
A real hard bone.

My helmet's connected to my
Cock bone,
My shaft is connected to the

Hard bone;

Boy, is it
   one big
      hard bone.
It's from
Dem bones,

Dem hard bones;

Dem bones,
Dem hard bones,

I get a real stiff hard bone
Now it a real bone-er!

(**Host PEEPING PECKER PETE comes back to the stage and has changed into a flashy suit with glittering jewels encrusted on the sleeves and front exterior. The glare is almost blinding.**) I just love the nightlife in the big city, don't'cha know… It's really a heap of fun. There are plenty of places to see and be seen, and you can always meet new people. There's a very special place which will be talked about in the next song. Let's meet that adorable little lavender boy himself, Prissy Bottoms, and give him a handjob --- ***ahem*** I mean, a BIG HAND, as he belts out his latest hit entitled, "Boystown."

BOYSTOWN

There's a place that is swinging,
The big cocks are flinging,
There's a place that you should go,
It's Boystown.

Drag queens are singing,
Closet queens are brought down to
Boystown.
Just take a look at the boy city,
Leave the nitty-gritty
And go to Boystown,
Down Boystown.

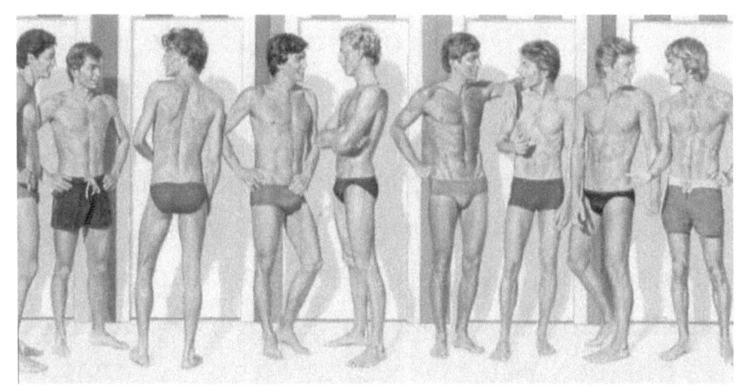

Bring a date or come single,
No one cares
As long as you mingle
Down in Boystown.
Boystown ---

Just look at all the glittery lights,
The dancing naked boys will hit ya
Right between the legs.
The lights, the cocks are big there,
You can forget about your hard-on pills
And go to Boystown,
Boystown!

Just check out all the boners,
It'll give you one
When you go down to Boystown,
Boystown.
So come one and all
And join me there in Boystown,
Boystown!!!

(**HOST shoos Prissy Bottoms off the stage with outrageous hand gestures. The singer sticks his nose in the air and goes off in a huff**.) I've had just about enough of that little twerp of a queen for one night, ladies and gentlemen. That reminds me: I just adore and admire performers who can dance. This next act fits the bill: expert singing and dancing. He's light on his feet. Let's welcome Tippy Thomasina, the greatest and lightest dancer of them all! He'll thrill you with his famous hit, "Skip Down, Trip Down." Listen closely to the message of this song --- they are words to live by, my friends!

SKIP DOWN, TRIP DOWN

**Skip down,
Trip down,
Come blow with me;
Come get down on the
Cock balls with me.
Way down,
Get on your knees,
You'll see
How happy you will be,**

**When you get down,
Trip down,
Come blow with me,
Come get down on the
Cock balls with me.**

Go up,
Down,
Way down
On your knees,
They'll love a
Good suck,
If you please.

So be sure to
Skip down,
Trip down,
Come blow with me;
Come get down on
the
Cock balls with me.

So when you need
A good blow,
You'll have a good
Suck-filled show,
Just be sure and
            simply....

Skip down,
Trip down,
Come blow with me;
Come get down on the
Cock balls with me.

There's nothing like listening to one of those old pirate tunes, right? Here's a group which'll sing their new hit. It's rising high up on the charts of degradation. Don't tell anybody, but it's sinking just as fast, too. Yuck-yuck! Here come all my mateys. You know them as The Jolly Rogers, and they'll be singing "The Monkey's Pecker." (**HOST rolls his eyes in disbelief as he walks offstage, mumbling under his breath, "This ought to be a real wiener!"**)

THE MONKEY'S PECKER

(spoken introduction)
Hey, me young mates,
Gather round and listen to
A story I was told.
Let me now tell ya,
If I may be so bold,
There was a little squirrely monkey
Who lived with all the shipmates.
The squirrely monkey doesn't like
Being caged up,
It's a fact.
He really hated it,
So one day something happened...

(begins singing chorus)
Oh, the monkey broke out

And got into the
Captain's pecker pills.
He took quite a lot,
He thought he was getting ill.
His little pecker began to grow
About a foot long out,
He began to shake it,
Dance around and shout!
He grabbed his cock,
It was hard as a rock.
He began whacking it off,
It was a sight to see.
This little squirrely monkey
Now has a very long, hard wee-wee.
This little squirrely monkey
Was showing it off
For all to see.
He was happy as he could be.

He once had a little pecker,
And now it's longer and bigger
Than you and me.
It was from when...
(go back to "Oh, the monkey broke out.."
    and repeat entire remainder of chorus.)

(Host PEEPING PECKER PETE struts back on stage to the rhythm of "The Monkey's Pecker" still playing in the background.) Isn't that the catchiest tune you've ever heard? I almost hate to introduce the next number because it may prove to be anticlimactic. At any rate, here's a group which needs no further introduction other than just to say, "Wank-Wank!" Ladies and Gentlemen, let's give a hearty round of applause for the one and only Hornettes!

WANK-WANK

There was once a horny fellow
Who loved to whip it out,
Especially when driving out and about.
He loved to go,
"Wank-wank, wank-wank!"
They guy went "wank-wank-wank!"

He did it very often,
Every chance he got;
He loved to "Wank-wank, wank-wank!"
The guy went "wank-wank-wank!"

One day he went driving,
He parked and went for a walk in the park.
He loved to show it off,
He was as happy as a lark.
He loved to go,
"Wank-wank, wank-wank!"

The guy went "wank-wank-wank!"

Until one day he took too many
Viagra pills,
"Wow!" he yelled to the top of his voice,
"They're giving me quite a thrill!"
They helped him go "wank-wank!"
But that day something went wrong,
He wanked off in front of an undercover cop.
Now he's no longer the Big Wanker,
But he sits in his cell, a-wankin' against the wall.
"Wank-wank, wank-wank!"
The guy goes "wank-wank-wank!"

Now he's learned his wanky lesson
As he whacks off in his home.
"Wank-wank!"
He loves to go "wank-wank!"

(HOST runs back to the stage, furiously rubbing his crotch. AUDIENCE members howl, whistle, scream and yell as PEEPING PECKER PETE takes a bow.) Ah, thank you, my friends. I must say I have more talent wanking my own wiener than all the big talk about it in that last song. And speaking of wieners, gang, there's a group of baseball-loving young guys who call themselves The Bally Boys. They're a brand new group, just formed shortly before our show went on the air today, and they'd like to premiere their first and only hit, none other than --- what else? --- "The Wiener Song." Let's give 'em a nice round of applause and listen closely to the important message contained in the lyrics of their song, OK? Take it away, Bally Boys!

THE WIENER SONG

Give me a big fat wiener,
One that is hard all the time;
One that does not get limp,
Standing up all the time.
Let me give it a stroke once or twice,
For it will feel mighty nice.

So give me a big fat wiener,
One that is hard all the time;
One that does not get limp,
But standing up all the time.
So whack-whack goes the wiener,
Boy, is it going to blow!

So give me a big fat wiener,
One that is hard all the time;
One that does not get limp,
Still standing up all the time.

It's easy to count as
One, two, three,
For there's nothing like a
Big fat wee-wee.
So give me a big fat wiener,
One that is hard all the time;
One that does not get limp,
Ever standing up all the time.

Aaaaallll....theeeeeee......TTTIIIIIMMMMMMEEE!!!

(PEEPING PECKER PETE is back onstage, sporting a pair of denim overalls and chewing on a corncob pipe stuck between his teeth.) You know, kiddies, we haven't had much representation on this show from the folk/rock community. You may not know it, but even I like to swing to a good country song ev'ry now and then, y'all. Here's one of my all-time favorites, interpreted for you and me by one of the best bands to ever grace this stage. I'm talkin' about The Cutie Boys, that's who! You're gonna find them --- where else? --- "Down on the Corner." Let's hear it for 'em, the Cutie Pie band!

DOWN ON THE CORNER

Down on the corner
Right on Lavender Street
There's a hot place
Where boys love to meet.

You can visit the Peep Show,
Just about a nickel or dime,
You can have your pick
Just about any ol' time.

It's down on the corner
Right on Lavender Street
There's a hot place
Where boys love to meet.

There's smoke, and coffee a-brewin'
Right inside "The Chain and Balls,"
They love to come in leather,
The men love a dark den.
If you love it rough inside
You can get a free whacking
On your hide.

It's down on the corner

Right on Lavender Street
There's a hot place
Where boys love to meet.

So come along,
come on down,
Don't bring any hangups,
You can often come in your
     diamond-studded
          leather pumps.

We'll see you
Down on the corner
Right on Lavender Street
There's a hip place
Where boys love to meet!

(HOST returns, wearing glasses with lenses shaped as stars) They say there's nothing like sitting under the bright moonlight and listening to a romantic song. One of our favorite groups, the Hornettes, are back to sing us another of their fabulous hits. This is one I'm sure you'll enjoy because it was a Number One song back in the day. Please feel free to sing along with the gals as they perform, "Coming In My Eyes."

COMING IN MY EYES

When you're feeling hot
You turn into a big sex pot
Wah-wah doobie-doo-wah
Shoobie-doobie....
When you're balls're on fire
You try to climax higher
But you come right in my eyes.

When you're about to cry
Climaxing in the night
Feels so incredibly right,
Wah-wah doobie-doo-wah

Shoobie-doobie....
When you're balls're on fire
You try to climax higher
But you come right in my eyes.

When your pecker pops
It squirts lots
It comes right in my eyes,
When your balls're on fire
You try to climax higher
But you come right in my eyes.
Shoobee-doo-waaaahhh-
        wah-wah.....!!

(HOST returns to the stage, wielding a huge set of tablets with Hebrew writing.) "Uff, those mothers sure are heavy! I dunno how them rabbis can carry those things around like they do. Just like I don't know why we can't have more Jewish acts on this show! To break that trend, we are honored to have the touring company from the Bella Abzug Yiddish Theatre and Kosher Deli in upstate New York with us here in the studio. They're gonna perform one of the many musical numbers from their highly successful off-Broadway novelty, "The Rabbi and the Showgirl." Here to sing that beloved show-stopping number, "A Big Hard One" is soloist Shlummie Schlubowitz. Take it away, Schlummie baby!

A BIG HARD ONE

If I ever had a long hard prick
Oh my, oh my, oh my, oh shit!
If I had a big stiffy, a really big one,
Oh, what miracles I could perform!

If I had one
I'd show it off,
I'd give thanks all the day.
If I had a big hard one ---

If I ever had a long hard prick
Oh my, oh my, oh my, oh shit!
I'd play with it and screw all day...

(speaking part) I have some words of wisdom:
            Oy vey, the Good Lord said
            "Be fruitful and multiply"
            So why not?

If I had a long hard prick
Oh my, oh my, oh my, oh shit!
I'd play and fiddle with my fiddle
All day long,
If I ever had a long hard prick.
Dee-dee, dah-dah, duhm!
I'd screw-y screw-y all day long....

(PEEPING PECKER PETE eyes a figure standing partially in the shadows in anticipation of the next act) Hmm,.... I see that some people are just too damn impatient. After that heavy dose of Yiddishkeit, we need to bring back a little gaiety in our lives. This next act reminds me of the days of burlesque. They're gonna perform a gem of a song for you. It's called "The Fairy Queen." Here they are for your approval, ladies and gentlemen, The Queenie Weenies!

THE FAIRY QUEEN

(emerging from the shadows is a slender young man wearing a diamond-studded jockstrap, painted toenails encrusted with sparkles and shiny studs, angel's wings and a black top hat)

Hey, everybody! Have you seen what
　　I've just seen?
There's nothing like it:
　　It's the Fairy Queen!

(lights flicker on, and a yell emerges
from offstage: "On with the show!")

Hey, everybody! Have you seen what
　　I've just seen?
There's nothing like it:

It's the Fairy Queen!

What an erotic turn-on!
He shakes it so sweet,
He has a hot ass
That really can't be beat!

So everybody, have you seen what
     I've just seen?
There's nothing like it:
     It's the Fairy Queen!

Romp and stomp along with him
     in your horny state,
I'd give him
A high rate ---

So hey everybody, have you seen what
     I've just seen?
There's nothing like it:
     It's the Fairy Queen!

(HOST carries a bow and arrow with him as he returns to the stage) Getting struck by Cupid's arrow is something we all experience at least once in our lives, right? With that in mind, my dear friends, let's listen to that high-stepping, high-strutting vocalist who has been delighting audiences with his songs for decades. He's a wrinkled old senior citizen these days, but he's still got that swingin' way about him! Ladies and Gentlemen, let's put our hands together and give a big round of applause to Stupid Cupid. He's gonna tell us all about that "Lavender Boy."

LAVENDER BOY

How I love my lavender boy,
Oh yeah, wow, doobie-doo-wah!
I loved you
When I picked
You up as my
   Trick
Oh, how you made my
   Prick
Stand up straight like a
   Stick!

Oh, how I love my lavender boy,
Oh yeah, wow, doobie-doo-wah!
I love the way you
Give me your little
   Smile,

Make my heart beat
Like running a
   Mile ---

Oh wow, oh wow,
I love how I love
My lavender boy,
Oh yeah, wow,
doobie-doo-wah!

My, how I love
Your bubbly butt,

You have me down
On my knees,
Wagging my tongue
Like an old
   Mutt.
Love licking your
Big juicy
Lollipop,
I love, I love, I love
My lavender boy,
Oh yeah, wow, doobie-doo-wah!

(**Host PEEPING PECKER PETE skips onto the stage and gushes sweetly**) I can never forget those wonderful games I played as a tyke growing up in the Midwest. What amazing times those were! With that in mind, here's a little number which recalls those fond days of times gone by when we kiddies romped to our heart's content in a carefree world. Dydee Down and His Dy-Nettes will now sing their monster hit for you, and we invite you to snap your fingers to the intoxicating rhythm!

TIE A PINK AND LAVENDER RIBBON
ROUND THE OL' PEE-PEE

Tie a pink and lavender ribbon
Round the ol' pee-pee
Please give it a jerk,
Make it hard for me.
You can just tie that
Pink and lavender ribbon
Round the ol' pee-pee ---

Bah-bee-wah-shoo-wop
Bah-bee-wah-shoo-pop
Bah-bee-wah-shoo-bop-bop....
Jerk-jerk!

I love when you get on it and
Sit on it,
Tease it if you please,
So long as you can wrap it
Round the ol' pee-pee.

I love it the most when you
Tie a pink and lavender ribbon

Round the ol' pee-pee.
So be sure to take some
        time out
When you're free
And have that pink and
        lavender ribbon
Tied round your ol'
        pee-pee.

Bobbie-wah-wah-jump-hump
Bobbie-wah-dah-boo-bop
Bobbie-wah-pop-pop...
And one last
        jerkity-jerkity-jerk!

(DYDEE DOWN and HIS DY-NETTES rush off the stage as they are stormed by a noisy group of motorcycles riding toward them with engines cranked up to ear-splitting levels. BRUTUS AND THE MACHO MEN alight from the bikes and menacingly sneer at the crowd of onlookers as they begin performing their musical number)

A HAPPY LEATHER BOY'S DITTY

Show, show, show your leather chaps
And acc-cess-sooo-ries
   for all to see
What a happy leather boy you'll be!

Whip, whip, crack your whip
And see how red and sore
   your ass will be!

Show, show, show your leather chaps
And acc-cess-sooo-ries
And oh! what a happy leather boy
   you will be!

Come, wear your leather clothes
And prepare to have your ass
   mightily whipped
With all of us leather men.

You'll just love our dark and
Dingy dungeon den.

Show off your leather chaps
And acc-cess-sooo-ries
For all to see,
What a happy leather boy you'll be!

(BRUTUS breaks away from the group
and points at the AUDIENCE members)
Before we leave this stage, I want all you
scumbags out there to join us in a final
chorus of our little song --- or else! All
together now (**Waves hands as if
directing a choir**)

Show off your leather chaps
And acc-cess-sooo-ries
For all to see,
What a happy leather boy
    you will be!

(**HOST is in a reflective mood. He comes back onstage, head bowed reverently and hand on chin, rubbing gently**). Every once in a while it's a good thing to stop and reflect about our lives: where we've been and where we're going. Most of all, thinking about all the regrets we have and the times we've really screwed up --- I mean, really, really fucked up big time. Here's Old Fart Dan, the old reminisce-er himself to sing a timely reminder about just how worthless our lives are. Hit it, Old Fart Dan, baby! Sing your greatest hit --- I can't stand listening it, but maybe the shitheels in the audience will like it --- you know, that one you call simply, "Young." Whew! What a stinker!

YOUNG

**When I was young
How often it rose and
How often I did cum....
A big head flying and
Sailing in the wind....**

**How I whacked it and
Jerked it all about;
When I did it,
I had no doubt.**

When I was
   young
How often it
   rose and
How often
   I did cum...
A big head flying
   and sailing
in the wind....
When I was young.

Now that I am old and gray,
It won't rise up or
Stay up all the day.
I wish I could get it up.
I try to play with it
As a horny little pup.

It's all when I was young...
How often it rose and
How often I did cum...
A big head flying and
Sailing in the wind...
When I was young...

(PEEPING PECKER PETE is shaking his head, disgusted by the depressing message of the last song, but willing to carry on in spite of it) I'm gonna need a good belt of something strong and adult to get over that piece of crap song from Old Fart Dan, but somehow I'll pull through. Maybe the next act'll pick me up. They're the Whacky Wanker Boys' Brigade and they'll be presenting one of their gems, a song I know you'll all enjoy. I have to admit, I sometimes suffer from the problem they're talking about in this song. Ladies and Gentlemen, please listen closely to the lyrics of "I Can't Get It Up."

I CAN'T GET IT UP!

Every morning
At the break of day
I hear that fucking music
A'playing in my head:
I can't get it up
I can't get it up
I can't get it up this morn-ning!

I can't get it up
No matter how much I try,
I can't get it up
No way.

I wish I had a big stiffy,
A big hard-on,

But I can't get it up
I can't get it up
I can't get it up this morn-ning!

No matter how much I try
I can't get it up
No way.

It's limp as my wrist,
Not stiffening at all.
I feel so frustrated,
I fondle both my balls
But no matter, it doesn't
Help at all.
So I sit here and sing to myself:

I can't get it up
I can't get it up
I can't get it up this morn-ning!

No matter how much I try
I can't get it up
No way.

(HOST dances back onstage, this time holding an umbrella which he flexes several times to the delight of the AUDIENCE members) Don't you just love those old-time musicals? You know, the ones with the lavish production numbers. We tried to duplicate one of those huge productions on this stage, but our producers are too damn stingy to finance anything like that. Instead, for your approval and enjoyment, we hired Trippytoes Joe, a cut-rate dancer from the burlesque. He's gonna sing and dance a lively little number for you called "Cumming in the Rain." I know you're gonna be thrilled to watch him trip the light fantastic. Take it away, Joe baby!

CUMMING IN THE RAIN

I'm cumming in the rain
What a glorious climax
I'm having again,
Love to do it when
I'm coming in the rain.

Cumming in the rain
I feel it's gonna
Happen again,
Like when it squirts out
And lands

Mixing with the rain.

It's all from
Cumming in the rain.
I'm cumming in the rain
What a glorious climax
I'm having again,
Love to do it when
I'm cumming in the rain.

Squirting again,
I feel like squirting again.
I love to do it
While I'm cumming in the rain.

So come on, let's whip it out
And give a "Hallelujah" shout
As we're both
Cumming in the rain.

It's just so much fun
When you're cumming in the rain.
Cumming in the rain...

(PEEPING PECKER PETE still holds his umbrella like before, flexing it several more times before tossing it completely offstage). Well, that was an uplifting song and dance number --- in more ways than one, if y'know what I mean, ladies and gentlemen --- yuck yuck! Our next act consists of a song by the Bouncy Gonads. They're fixin' to tell us about a problem all of us have had to put up with at one time or another: namely, "My Red Rubber Balls." Come on out here, Bouncy Gonads, and show us your stuff!

MY RED RUBBER BALLS

I never felt this way at all
It turns red when I feel them
There's nothing like the look and feel
Of my red rubber balls.

It feels so fine
Just putting 'em out in the sun
Makes them shine
There's nothing like my
Red rubber balls.

Stop, look at them,
Shake and whack them,
See how they bouncey-bounce,
Oh! How I love my red rubber balls.

Host PEEPING PECKER PETE enters the stage before the members of BOUNCY GONADS have the chance to exit. He grabs one of the musicians from the band, forces him to bend over and positions himself right over the poor guy, locking him in a tight embrace while making obscene humping motions against the man's backside.) Thanks to my buddy here, I have the perfect introduction for our next brilliant musical offering: none other than one of the great singers and songwriters of our era, Horny Hamill. He'll be performing his gargantuan million-selling hit, "The Hump." Before I release him, let's give our friend here from the Bouncy Gonads a round of applause for being such a good sport and allowing me to hump him as I introduced Horny's great song. (AUDIENCE breaks out in thunderous applause, cheers and catcalls. The embarrassed musician runs offstage, cursing and yelling at HOST: "Don't ever do that to me again, Buster!")

THE HUMP

C'mon babe, let's do the hump!
C'mon everyone, let's do the hump!
You can do it like
You're screwin',
Using your rump.
We're gonna hump till we screw
The house down.

C'mon let's hump, honey, hump!
Like you're screwin' with your rump.

You can do it when nobody's around,
Just get atop your partner,
You'll begin to rock.
Start to hump, baby, hump!
That's right!
When you're tight,
You'll feel right
When you hump.

Yeah, yeah,
I feel like it's a-cummin'
Gonna blow the roof off!
So c'mon, join me –
Let's hump, sugar, hump!
Ooooh waaaah
Let's hump!

We're gonna hump the night away,
Just join me and
Do the hump!

(HOST runs back onstage, holding a gigantic lollipop with colorful swirls and licking it with glee) And now for all you kiddies out there, a cute little song about a special ship on the high seas which always sails chockful of sweet goodies for all good little girls and boys: none other than "The Hot Ship Cockenpop." And one of the most beautiful, buxomest sailors is gonna sing it for ya: your favorite salty sea dog and mine, the fabulous Sexy Sadie!

THE HOT SHIP COCKENPOP

On the hot ship Cockenpop
It's a nice place
Where you cum a lot
Where you eat and suck on
Peppermint cocks
While you sail on your way.

It's all on the hot ship Cockenpop
Where the flavored cocks are hard as rocks
While sailing on your way.

You can eat your fill
You don't pay a big bill
It's all free
On the hot ship Cockenpop.
It's a nice place
Where you cum a lot
Where you eat and suck on peppermint cocks
While you sail on your way-aaayyyyy!

(**HOST returns to stage wearing a huge sombrero and a gaudy sarape, shaking a pair of maracas as he walks. He begins belting out a few words in Spanish)** "*La cucaracha, la cucaracha, ya no puede caminar...*" Oh, I just love a nice Mexican hat dance. This next act is lively, ladies and gentlemen, I hope you can keep up with him. He's a real jumping bean of a guy, none other than that jolly tamale himself, Racy Rodriguez! (**HOST mutters to himself as he walks offstage**, "Hmm..., think I'll have myself a walking taco while he's on!")

THE LIMBER COCK

Pull it once or twice
Make it feel real nice
Bounce it once
Give it some spice
It's like rocking around the clock
Hey, let's do the Limber Cock!

La-la-la, la-la
It's so unique
Makes you feel real chic
Hey, let's do the Limber Cock!

So, whip it, pull it out,
Whack it as you give a shout!
It's no doubt
You'll have fun when you
Do the Limber Cock.

C'mon, join the fun
You can do it in the sun
Let's go and do
The Limber Cock!

Are you ready?
How limber can your cock go....?
You can yank it,
Pull it,
Go ahead,
Grab a handful,
Let's go!

La-la-la-la la-la-la,
How much longer is your cock?
Let's do the Limber Cock!
Ay-yay-yay-yay-yay!
Hee-hahhh!

(**HOST runs back on stage, drops his pants and causes total mayhem among the AUDIENCE members. When they recover from their shock, he pulls his pants back up and continues with his duties as emcee**) I guess we all get a little shocked now and then, right, gang? I saw how you reacted to me dropping my pants here on our stage. I had an ulterior motive, though. It was to prepare you for the next act: a really bawdy song with lyrics so explicit, they'll curl your hair. You guessed it: it's none other than The Harlots, that great group of hair-curling gals themselves, and they're gonna tell you the saga of "The Old Gray Fart Knocker." I know it'll tear at your heartstrings, maybe even give you a few chuckles. Take it away, girls!

THE OLD GRAY FART KNOCKER

I've been to bed with men before,
Some of them were really hot;
But there was one who really
Made me laugh a lot;
He claimed he screwed many a girl
And was so hot to trot;
But when I was alone with him
He couldn't even get it in;
For the old gray fart knocker
Couldn't get it up
Couldn't get it up,
He couldn't even get it in.

You should've seen it,
It was quite a scene;
He was something else
Never a man has there been;
He came in, dropped his pants,
Began to jerk it all about;
But that poor thing of his
He couldn't get it up.
The old gray fart knocker
Couldn't get it up
Couldn't get it up,
He couldn't even stick it in.

I feel so sorry for him,
He thought he was such a big stud;
But a prick like his
Went limp as a dud
Because the old gray fart knocker
Couldn't get it up,
Couldn't get it up,
He couldn't even keep it up.

My goodness, he couldn't screw
Because he couldn't get it in;
He's the old gray fart knocker who
Couldn't get it in,
And couldn't even find it,
Let alone get it in!

(HOST comes back to the stage, sporting a huge plastic nose over his real one) Hey, everybody! Whad'ya think of this nose, huh? Pretty schnozzy…I mean, schnazzy! It began growing bigger as I started thinking about our next guest performer on this naughty, bawdy musical spectacular. It must've gotten aroused, if you get my drift --- yuck yuck! Let's all welcome that nosy old vaudevillian himself, the immortal Pecky Peckeroonie, singing his most beloved hit song, "A Pecker-Dee, A Pecker-Doo." Take it away, Pecky!

A PECKER-DEE, A PECKER-DOO

Hey, a pecker-dee, a pecker-doo, a pecker-dee ---
How d'ya like this big schozz o' mine?
It's as big as a pickled pecker, huh?
I've pickled --- oops, I mean *tickled*
      many a date with this one!

Hey, a pecker-dee, a pecker-doo, a pecker-dee ---
My pecker's hard when it's a pecker-dee
Because it's hard for you and me,

A pecker-doo
Is when I love doing it with you,
It's with my pecker-dee that I
Pecker-doo!

My pecker's hard just for you!
A pecker-dee, a pecker-doo
It's all for you!

It's a pecker-dee, a pecker-doo,
You know I've got a million
Peckers for you!

(shuffles off stage, motioning with his cane and
tipping his hat)

(HOST struts back on stage) I love folk music, and this next artist has a huge array of hits in that musical genre. We only have time for one song, though, and we've picked a doozy: "Going Down on You." It's guaranteed to take you down, and I'm talking about waaaa-y down. In fact, this song had been goin' down ever since the guy recorded it. Let's give a big hand to Shaun Pawnypuss as he sings "Going Down on You."

GOING DOWN ON YOU

As you go down
As you go down
As you go down
On your knees
A-going down
The world's spinning round
While your hot pecker lips
On me
Are going down

It's a going down,
Up and down,
Love the stroking
On it
As you're going down.

So let's go down,
Go way down,

Slide up and down
As we're going down,
Love it all
When we're all
Going down,
We're a-going down
On me.

So let's go down
As the world goes down
Let the world spin round
As you're going down
On me.

(HOST comes out in a red and black checkered lumberjack shirt, his thumbs pegged on the straps of the same baggy bib overalls he was wearing to introduce an earlier number. This time, however, he isn't chewing on the end of a corncob pipe) Folk music has been the backbone of America. And you've got to admit, ladies and gentlemen, that some of our best and brightest folk artists have been big --- really big! To illustrate my point, here are those fabulous big folk singers themselves, The Three Naughty Ones. They're gonna interpret their really big hit which is appropriately called, "If I Had a Big One."

IF I HAD A BIG ONE

If I had a big one
I'd wank it in
    the morning ,
I'd stroke it
    in the evening
All of the time

I'd whack it till it's creamy,
It's feels ever so dreamy,
If I had a big one
Covering all of my hand
Ooooh-ooooh, ooooh-ooooh.

If I had a big one
I'd whip it out all of the time,
Love it when it's a hard one,

Oh, it looks so fun.
If I had a big one
I'd wank it in the morning,
I'd stroke it in the evening
All of the time

I'd whack it till it's creamy
It's feels so dreamy
All of the time.
Ooooh-ooooh, ooooh-ooooh.

So I'll continue to
Wank it in the morning,
I'll stroke it in the evening
All of the everloving time ---
It'll make me free
And so happy
If I had one to wank
All of the time....
Ooooh-ooooh, ooooh-ooooh,
Yeah, yeah, yeah!

(HOST reappears onstage, but is in silhouette) You see me like this, all of your in the audience and out there in TV land, because our next act is as shadowy as their name. They are The Shadowy Wankers and they're gonna sing for you the song you've all breathlessly been waiting for: "Me and My Cock'n'balls." You'll enjoy it, beyond a shadow of a doubt!

ME AND MY COCK'N'BALLS

Me and my cock'n'balls
Waving and wanking all the day
Every day
In every way
It's feeling so hard.

Doo-dee-doo

So me and my cock'n'balls
Waving and wanking all the day
I yank it
Jerk it
Never ever hurt it
It's such a hard one
It's all because of
Me and my cock'n'balls
Waving and wanking all the day
They're such close friends
They're always there

Even while I'm bare
Because of me and my cock'n'balls
Waving and wanking all the day

They're looking and
Feeling okay
Every day
In every way
They make me feel great
All the day.

That's me and my cock'n'balls
Waving and wanking all the day

Doo-dee-doo, doo-dee-doo, doo-dee-doo....
(music fades)

(**PEEPING PECKER PETE has donned a Polynesian grass skirt and holds a ukulele**) The Cockabee Islanders have flown over from their home in Whack-ki-ki to present this lovely little traditional Hawaiian ditty for us tonight. It's entitled, "The Pecker and I' and I know you're all gonna treasure it forever and ever. Let's shout a great big "Aloha!" and give a nice, generous round of applause to them: the Cockabee Islanders!

THE PECKER AND I

The pecker and I
We both can sway and
Swing in the breeze.
It feels like such a tease!
It's my pecker and I ---
La-la-la-la-la-la-la,
My pecker and I.

My, what a feeling,
It's three-ling!
It's my pecker and I,
My pecker and I ---

La-la-la-la-la-la-la

My cock is so sweet,
Just love wanking it and
Giving it a beat.
I give thanks to my
My pecker and I,
My pecker and I ----
La-la-la-la-la-la-la

It's really quite unique
It's my pecker and I!
La-la-la-la-la-la-la-la-la!!

(stage lights dim, ready for the huge gala closing
number. All of the performers from the previous
acts have assembled and sing a chorus along with
special guest vocalist, SMUTTY MUTT)

THERE'S NO BUSINESS LIKE SEX BUSINESS

There's no business like sex business,
Everybody gets that horny feeling,
They love getting a good plow,
Even if you're a beginner
You'll learn how!
You'll be sure to get your cherry popped.

I fucked an unmarried virgin
(VOICES shout: "You'll hang for that!")
'Cause there's no business like sex business,
Everybody gets that horny feeling,
They love to go get plowed,
Even if you're a beginner,
You'll have your cherry popped, and how!

There's nothing like the sex business,
You'll grab your balls when you get
That hanging, lowdown feeling,
You'll find yourself at a peep show,
So there's no business like sex business
Everybody gets that horny feeling,
And you'll be sure to get a good plow,

Even if you're a beginner,
Your time is now!

So come and join the sex business,
You'll enjoy our peep show,
There's nothing like it
To give you a hard bone.
It makes you grab your balls
When you are low…
There's nothing like the turn-on feeling
As you climax with
A moan and groan!

And so there's no business like sex business,
Let's enjoy the sex business, one and all
Including those balls
'Cause there's nothing like
                the sex business
                        for all!

(**PEEPING PECKER PETE emerges
from the crowd of performers,
holding his arms out as if to take in
the entire studio with his grasp --- a
corny yet effective gesture, to be
sure. He smiles, waves and shouts at
the AUDIENCE)** That wraps up our
show for tonight, ladies and
gentlemen as well as to all you lovely
viewers out there watching us on
your TV sets in the comfort of your
own crummy homes. We'll be back
with another special real soon --- I
hope to God not TOO soon, but soon
enough, I'm sure. In the meantime,
take care and stay sexy!

If you enjoyed this book, you might also like

Available in paperback and Kindle formats

at

www.esmeraldalintner.net

and all Amazon sites worldwide
Simply search "ESMERALDA LINTNER"

www.ingramcontent.com/pod-product-compliance
Lightning Source LLC
Chambersburg PA
CBHW020747160726
47993CB00006B/2651